Roses and Soul

"Roses and Soul"

ISBN No: " 978-93-91302-20-7"
1st Edition
Language – English and Hindi

Flairs and Glairs
Publication House
Regd. Under MSME Act.

Disclaimer

This is a work of fiction and solely represent the thoughts of the corresponding authors of the articles. Our editors have tried their best to edit the content of all the authors and check the plagiarism.

All the write-ups in this book are unique and are only published in this book.

In case any plagiarism or error is found, only the author is responsible alone, and not the publisher or the Compilers.

Cover Designing and Book Formatting

Shubham Shah and Ishani Agarwal

Acknowledgment

Dear God, thank you for your blessings,
Also thanks to my family they did everything for me. The compilation of this anthology would have not been possible with the support of Co-authors. A very big thanks to all the Co-authors and the entire team who have been working with us and gave their precious time to us. Special thanks to Shubham Shah and Ishani Agarwal
for guiding me and supporting me although. A good editor makes an ordinary book attractive, thank you Grishma Ninave for doing that. And also thanks to Garima Batra and Shivangi
Jaiswal for helping me get co-authors for this
anthology. And lastly, I Thank "Flairs and Glairs" whole team for helping me.
Thank you all of you for being there.

Co Authors

Shubham Shah (Founder Flairs and Glairs)
Ishani Agarwal (Co-Founder Flairs and Glairs)
Riya Rashmi Dash (Compiler)

1. Sandeep Chamola
2. आयुषी शर्मा "आयु"
3. Vaibhav Gupta
4. Sahil Hindustani
5. Sakshi Jain
6. Monisha.T
7. Kalamkaar
8. Anand jain
9. Padma Srivastava
10. Urvi Gajjar
11. Nikhil Jain
12. Kristi Dutta
13. Vikrant Singh
14. Suchismita Ghoshal
15. मनोज शर्मा
16. Krishna Motwani
17. Jayashree Sahoo
18. Panalcherin Wekesa
19. Ryan Sean
20. Tabassum Hasnat
21. Rashmika
22. Ashish Verma
23. Hershey's
24. Parul Mishra
25. Pratham Mittal

26. Diksha Motwani
27. Debarati Das
28. Sakshi Sharma
29. Srishty Singh
30. Ananya Mohanty
31. Abdul Hasan
32. Mahi Adlakha
33. Supriya Mukherjee
34. Preetam Khatua
35. Mani Prasad Kar
36. Archishman Satpathy
37. Surekha Wankhede
38. Riddhi Gupta
39. Ganesh Sadashiv Patil
40. Kinjal Patel
41. Vedika Shukla
42. Merlin Dorcus
43. Nilanjana Sarkar
44. Arun Pratap Singh
45. Irene Joseph
46. Shaik Moiden S
47. Kirti Goel
48. V.Dhanashree
49. Anshuk Dwivedi'ranghin
50. Chirag L Sagar

Shubham Shah

(Founder- Flairs and Glairs)

Shubham Shah, an entrepreneur at "Flairs & Glairs" a brand with dynamics in events organizing and cultural educational pan INDIA, is a 26yrs old guy who recently has entered the digital platform of imprinting emotions. He has initiated with his own open mic platform to help budding poets and aspiring writers under his brand named as "Teekhe Zasbaaat"

He is a commerce graduate from the Bhagalpur City of Bihar.

He states Writing has impersonated him since childhood and he has now been writing for over a decade!

Cooking, on the other hand, is his passion! He also mentions, trying out new things just tickles him!

When asked sir, Why SPICY EMOTIONS?

He smiled and added, "agar jasbaat teekhe na ho toh wo jasbaat kahan" Spices are all that blends! So do his words!

As a chef, he presents to you his dish! Hot and freshly served! Taste it! Feel it! Enjoy it! You can also find his writing in the Book "Teekhe Zasbaaat" and 50+ Co-authored anthologies. With his passion to explore opportunities across Platforms, he is working with keen devotion and We wish him all the very best for his future ventures.

He is Featured in the International Magazine DeMode for his upcoming solo novel.

He is Approved by Ne8x for its Lit Fest, and is a Golden Star Awards 2020 Winner.

He is a India Book of Records Holder for his Anthology Satrang, and has the Grandmaster title by Asia Book of Records, for the same.

He has also been featured in Prabhat Khabar, Dainik Jagran, and a lot of other Newspapers in Bihar for his achievements.

He has been a proud co-author to

India Book Of Records (Title- Black)

World Book Of Records (Title -15 Wonders of Poetries)

India Book Of Records (Title - Aaina)

Vajra World Records Holder (Title - Gustakhi Maaf Hai)

High Range of Records Holder (Title - Gustakhi Maaf Hai)

Indian Book of Records

(Title - Road from Worst to Best)

Share your reviews on his

INSTAGRAM

@spicy_emotions
@shubham4shah

Or via email on

shubham2shah@gmail.com

To stay tuned to his work and opportunities follow his business Handles

INSTAGRAM FACEBOOK YOUTUBE

@flairsandglairs
@teekhezasbaaat

WEBSITE:

https://flairsandglairs.in/
https://flairsandglairs.com/

Ishani Agarwal

(Co-Founder- Flairs and Glairs)

Ishani Agarwal hails from the City of Joy, Kolkata.
She is the co-founder of her Community "Teekhe Zasbaaat" and Flairs and Glairs Publication.
Been a Compiler for 45+ Anthologies, she is in the process for more. Co-authored in 150+ Anthologies. She is a India Book of Records Holder, a Vajra World Records Holder, a High Range of Records Holder, an OMG Book of Records Holder, a Bravo Record holder, a Forever Star Book of World Records and an Indian Book of Records Holder.
Approved by Ne8x for its Lit Fest 2020, and Literary Icon 2020. Also a Golden Star Awards Winner 2020.
She has also been awarded with India Star Republic Award 2021, a part of She Awards by Awards Arc and Winner of Nari Samman 2021 by Literoma.

She is also selected as Best Achiever of the Year by AwardsArc and Most Challenging Compiler Award by Spectrum Awards.
She got her first solo Published,a solo Compilation consisting of first 750 contents of hers, titled "Hand That Burnt While Healing".

She has been featured by the National Magazine "Taree Zameen Par" with the title 'unstoppable'.
Also featured in the International Magazine DeMode for her upcoming solo novel, she is proud to write on social issues, and is happy with the love she is receiving.
Connect with her on Instagram: @Ishani_agarwal_quotes / @compilations_so_far

Compiler
Riya Rashmi Dash

She is Riya rashmi dash presently pursuing her BBA from KIIT University, Bhubaneswar. She is Selenophile, loves to enjoy every small moment of her life, and is a wanderlust. She is a writer and started her passion 2 years back and also aspires to be future HR Manager. She has worked in more than 100 anthologies as co-author and compiler of 6 books till now and more ongoing. She is also the Author of her solo book"Waiting to Exhale"She is also been part of national magazines, featured in author interview, part of world record books. She is the Founder of The Opus Coliseum and is happy as her life is turning out now and hopes this continues as such.

Insta- _riyaa_rashmi

Sandeep Chamola

Sandeep chamola is an Engineer from uttarakhand
He is passionate for his writing works and experience for 1 year in writing. He wins many contest by his skills of writing .He is intrested to write in shayri ,quotes,Gazal, and much more .

INSTAGRAM:- S_A_N_D_E_E_P__C_H_A_M_O_L_A The_silent_tales.7

मेरी तो अभी ग़ज़ल चल रही है

उम्मीद ज़िन्दगी की ढल रही है,
यादें सहमी है मगर मचल रही है।
कड़वाहट कुछ बाकी है नजाने क्यों
मेरी तो अभी ग़ज़ल चल रही है।

मुझसे काफी दूर बसेरा ठहरा तुम्हारा
क्या दूरी से तुम्हारी ज़िन्दगी सम्भल रही है
तुम ऐश में बिताना ज़िन्दगी अपनी ,
मेरी तो अभी ग़ज़ल चल रही है।

हज़ारों भीड़ में लाखों शहर में
मगर तू मेरे दिल में चल रही है
तेरे वक़्त ने तुझे मंज़िल दिला दी
मेरी तो अभी ग़ज़ल चल रही है।

हवाएँ शर्द मौसम बेरुखा सा,
है तू सामने मेरी यादें पिघल रही हैं।
ज़माना चाँद पर जा पहुंचा
मेरी तो अभी ग़ज़ल चल रही है

सन्नाटा गहरा शोर लफ़्ज़ों में दबा
क्या कहने तेरे नाम से जुबां फिसल रही है,
अब तो घर में शहनाई आँगन में तेरे बारात आ गयी,
मेरी तो अभी ग़ज़ल चल रही है।

आयुषी शर्मा "आयु"

She is Ayushi Sharma and she lives in roorkee. She is doing her phd but she is a writter by her heart. She is co author in many books. Ayushi loves to help animals.
INSTAGRAM:- ayushi.0207

आज फोन पर तेरी आवाज़ आ गयी

सूनी विरान दुनिया में चहक आ गयी
आज फोन पर तेरी आवाज़ आ गयी
तेरे सूखे दिल पर मोहब्बत की बरसात आ गयी
आज फोन पर तेरी आवाज़ आ गयी
मेरे उदास चेहरे पर मानो सालो बाद मुस्कान आ गयी
आज फोन पर तेरी आवाज़ आ गयी
छुपी थी जो आँखो में बाहर वो नमी आ गयी
आज फोन पर तेरी आवाज़ आ गयी
मेरे तरसते कानो को अपने नाम की पुकार आ गयी
आज फोन पर तेरी आवाज़ आ गयी
काम मेरे दुआओ की आज शक्ति आ गयी
आज फोन पर तेरी आवाज़ आ गयी

साथ नहीं छोड़ा

आज भी साथ हैं हम क्योंकि मैने हाथ नहीं छोड़ा
मैने अपने प्यार का साथ नहीं छोड़ा
तुने तो अपने ज़ज़्बातो को दबा लिया था खुद में
मगर मैने अपने अलफ़ाज़ो से तुझे मनाना नहीं छोड़ा
ना जाने क्यों छोटी बातों पर अलग हो गया तू मुझसे
मगर मैने इतना होने पर भी अपना कोई वादा नहीं तोड़ा
तुने अपने रास्ते बदलने जब चाहे मुझसे
मैने अपने प्यार का सफ़र नहीं छोड़ा
आज भी साथ हैं हम क्योंकि मैने हाथ नहीं छोड़ा
मैने अपने प्यार का साथ नहीं छोड़ा

Vaibhav Gupta

This is Vaibhav Gupta belonging to Kanpur, UP. He is a graduate and had working in hospitality department . He has keen interest in poetries and stories. He has recently authored the e-novel "it happend in delhi" and is working on few more. Besides, He has been actively participating on events those lead him to his passion.

INSTAGRAM:- thevaibhav_gupta

Emotions

•

I wanna say I just want you,
I wanna say that i need you.
I need you to live,
I need you to breathe,
I need you to awake
And I need you to sleep.

You are my happy zone,
Without you I'm alone,
You know what I mean,
Have you ever been so keen,
To live a life with full of joy,
You know you are my soft toy.

Just want you to know,
I'm never wanna let you go,
We will do a big fight,
Until you hug me tight,
To realize the motions,
Your heart and my emotions..

Sahil Hindustani

His name is Sahil Bhatnagar born in Udaipur, Rajasthan in Febuary 1988. He writes under pen name SAHIL HINDUSTANI, given by his father. He is writing poems and stories since August 2004.

He had first listened to 'Dr. Vishnu Saxena' and read gazals of 'Mirza Galib' . So his write-ups (poems of romanticism) has glimpses of urdu words.

Few of his poems are published in different magazines and paper.He owns a youtube channel, named 'the super s sahil'.

INSTAGRAM:- sh_abc

कहने को

तुझमे मुझको दिखता रब
लड़की है तू कहने को

तेरे लब़ों से पीता मय़
ज़ाहिद तो हूँ कहने को

साँसें-धड़कनें मेरी तो तेरी
मेरी तो वो कहने को

तेरे लिए रहता बेसबर
सब्र मुझमे बस कहने को

एक तेरा ही ध्यान मुझे
अपना तो बस कहने को

तू ही मेरा है ख़ुदा
शिव-विष्णु तो कहने को

हाए क्या बात है

मुस्कुराती आ रही जो वस्ल के लम्हात है
मीठा खंज़र चला रही हाए क्या बात है

घायल करती मुझे उसके पायल की छनकार है
दौड़ कर आई है पास हाए क्या बात है

मद भरी ये रात है ऊपर से बरसात है
एसे में तेरा आना हाए क्या बात है

तेरी सादग़ी के आगे आराइश भी मात है
तेरे मन की सुंदरता की भी हाए क्या बात है
आराइश - सुंदरता

तेरे आने से हर रात लगती पूनम की रात है
तेरे उजले मुखड़े की भी हाए क्या बात है

हम तुम दोनों चुप बस गूंज रही बयार है
नज़रों से नज़रें पाती सुरूर हाए क्या बात है

Sakshi Jain

She is Sakshi Jain from Roorkee, Uttarakhand. She is pursuing B.A.Sociology from her hometown. She is a clever child and never tend to quit in life. She is a life - fighter. She loves Writing and dancing.

INSTAGRAM:- sakshijain_writes.

The Love Of A Child

They're not looking for perfection,
You're are their parent; their all.
They just want to know they're loved .
And that you'll come when they call.
They don't look at you in horror;
When you haven't brushed your hair .
In fact, they don't care what you look like ;
They just love that you are there.
They look to you for answers,
Perhaps a million questions a day,
Because you're their source of wisdom.
So it matters what you say;
It's not about status
Of diamonds and gold.
It's about genuine smiles,
And a warm hand to hold.
And they look to you for kindness;
For unconditional love
You are Mum.
You are Dad.
You are more than Enough.

Monisha.T

She is Monisha. A daughter of Thirunavukkarasu and Reena.
She is currently lived in Villupuram.
She is 18 years of age. She done her Bachelor degree in Physics.
She participate more than 50 anthology as a co-author.
In her every write-ups contains one beautiful concept.
Her words are coming from her kind heart.
She love herself very much.
INSTAGRAM:- monisha_t_official

Heart To Heart

You came in my dream while I was sleeping
You came as medicine for my wound
You came as an umbrella for my showers
You came as an angle to my eyes
You came as flower on my way
So I came to see you with a flower…
You disappeared somewhere when
You know I was coming….!
I'm looking for you to mix with the wind…
The flower in my hand may have withered
At the time I was looking but I never withered….
I looking forward to seeing you with
The withered flower….
When will you came to see me…?

Kalamkaar

This is Kalamkaar. He is from Uttrakhand bought up in Meerut(Up). His hobbies are reading and writing. His interest is in writing. He love writing. He is part of 295 +Anthologies as Co-Author. He won 290 + Certificate in Writing, He Start writing 29 February 2020. He is part of 2 anthology as Co Author going for record and He is omg record holder as Co - Author of Book Called Laposia. He is part of 4 international Anthologies as Co – Author. He is simple and people observer. He believes in Karma.

INSTAGRAM:- Kalamkaar51

पहला प्यार

जब मिलती हैं निगाहे उससे तो सब कुछ धुंदला लगता हैं !
आती नहीं नींद और खयालो उसके फिर वो जगता है !
जैसे लगता हैं सब कुछ सुहाना हैं !
उसके सिवा नहीं किसी का दिल मे आना हैं !
दिखने के लिए उसको किसी बहाने से उसके घर जाना हैं !
और होजाता उसका वो दीवाना हैं !
फिर बात करने के लिए किसी बहाने से हिम्मत जुटाना |
फिर हिम्मत करके उससे बात करना, बात करके अपने इश्क़ का इज़हार करना |
और सातवे आसमान मे ख़ुद को पाना |
जब अपने दिल - o-अज़ीज़ को पा लेना |
उससे सारी बाते करना, उसकी फिक्र जाताना |
उसको प्यार भरे नामो से पुकारना |
अपनी हमेशा पलकों पे बिठाना |
अगर कुछ दफ़े के लिए बात ना करें तो नाराज़गी जाताना ¡|
उसकी मासूमियत पे सब कुछ हार जाना |
नाराज़गी भुलाकर उसको सीने से लगाना |
उसकी पसंद की सारी चीज़े करना !
उसको खोने से डरना !
होता हैं कुछ अलग ही भूत सवार !
ऐसा होता हैं पहला प्यार !

रहना तुम्हारे बिना दुस्वार हैं!
तुम्हारे सिवा नहीं किसी से प्यार हैं!
भटक रहा हु दर बदर ढूढ़ता हुआ तुमको
उठा रहा हु तुमको पाने के लिए कई सितम!

Anand Jain

ANAND JAIN is a good writer from FAZILKA, PUNJAB
He has completed his GRADUATION in commerce stream. From Panjab University.
He has been writing poetry for 3 years as his passion. With the help of sister (sapna jain) and brother (Rakesh jain).
He wants to be a successful banker in future.
He is a founder of ROBIN HOOD ARMY, FAZILKA (NGO).
INSTAGRAM:- Anand_jain_12

शरारत

तेरी आँखों के सब आँसू मेरी आँखों में रहते हैं! मुहब्बत ये नहीं, तो फिर मुहब्बत किसको कहते हैं !!

नज़ारा कुछ हो सामने, नज़र में तुम ही रहते हो! इबादत ये नहीं, तो फ़िर इबादत किसको कहते हैं !!

तुम सामने मेरे हो, पर हो अजनबी जैसे कोई ! क़यामत ये नहीं, तो फ़िर क़यामत किसको कहते हैं !

खफ़ा हो, फिर भी बैठे हो मेरे पहलू से तुम सट कर!
शरारत ये नहीं, तो फ़िर शरारत किसको कहते हैं !!

तुम ऐसे मुस्कुराते हो के साँसे रुक सी जाती हैं ! तमाज़त ये नहीं, तो फ़िर तमाज़त किसको कहते हैं !!

सुकूँ मिलता है बस मुझको तेरी बाँहों के घेरे में। अक़ीदत ये नहीं, तो फ़िर अक़ीदत किसको कहते हैं !!

तेरी आँखों के रस्ते से तेरे दिल में उतरना है 'आनंद'।
मसाफ़त ये नहीं, तो फिर मसाफ़त किसको कहते हैं !!

तुम और चांद

है असर तेरे नाम का, ज़हनों-दिल पर कुछ ऐसा, हों भले ही आँखे नम, पर मुस्कुरा के लिखते हैं...

ठहर गयी है ज़िन्दगी, अब तुम से तुम तक ही, अब जब भी लिखते हैं, तुमको ही यारा लिखते हैं...

मुझसे ज्यादा प्यार तुम्हे, तुम खुद भी ना करते होंगे, कुछ ऐसे समझो की तुमको हम, तुमसे चुरा कर लिखते हैं...

प्यारे-प्यारे ख्वाबों में, भरकर अपनी बाहों में, हम दिसंबर की रातों में, तुम्हे नींद भुला कर लिखते हैं...

तुमसे ज़्यादा अज़ीज़ नही कुछ, तुम प्यार से भी प्यारे हो, तुमको चाँद सा प्यारा नही, हम चाँद को तुम सा लिखते हैं...

तुमसे ज़्यादा ना चाहा कुछ, तुमसे ज़्यादा क्या चाहेंगे, खुदा कसम तुम को हम, सजदे बराबर लिखते हैं...

Padma Srivastava

She is Padma Srivastava, born and brought up in varanasi and started writing from the age of 13year. She is a student of Pg from Archaeology from Banaras Hindu University with it she is also a good writer and singer. She became graduated from Banaras Hindu University, Varanasi. She is fond of singing and writing and composing poetry from starting. She started her career in writing as a co _author since July 2020 from flairs and glairs publication. Now she has been co _author of several anthologies.

INSTAGRAM:- _s_unknown_feelings

न जाने ये कैसी उम्मीदें जोड़ रहीं हू, पता है खतरनाक हैं वो राहें
फ़िर भी ख़ुद को उसी ओर मोड़ रहीं हूँ,
जोड़ा था बड़ी मुश्किल से फिर से वो नाता तोड़ रहीं हूं
थोड़ा अजीब थोड़ा ख़ुशनुमा सीधी राह का पता ही नहीं
अजीबोगरीब तो ये इश्क़ का चाल सा है
कोई इश्क़ से परेशान कोई दर्द में डूबा
हर गली में तो ये बना बवाल सा है
मोहब्बत नहीं ये नफरतों का जाल सा है ,
जो भी कहो पर ये रिश्ता बड़ा कमाल का है ,,,
कहीं है शहर में तन्हाई का मंज़र तो
कहीं सन्नाटा भी खड़ा सवाल सा है बस कुछ दिनों से चल रहा हमारे
मोहब्ब्त का यही हाल सा है
वफ़ादारी से भरी मोहब्ब्त हो,
शक का फीका रंग ना लगने पाए,
ये किस्मत का तोहफा नहीं तो क्या है ,
सब कुछ है पर वो नहीं तो
ये लकीरें खफ़ा नहीं तो क्या है,
हर बार अधुरा ही रह जाता है ये खेल इश्क़ का,
ये होता हर दफा नहीं तो क्या है
हो पीठ पीछे हाथ मे खंजर, है दर्द बना
इश्क़ उसका मगर ये दगा नहीं तो क्या है
खुद है वाकिफ़ उसके रग रग से,
पर कोई कुछ बोले उसे ये मंज़ूर नहीं,
ये वफ़ा नहीं तो क्या है। ।

Urvi Gajjar

Urvi Gajjar is a 21 years old young author, graduated in commerce Born in Maharashtra (Mumbai),. Her innovative ideas, loving heart and the enthusiasm towards literature brimmed her personality with the shining pearls of beautiful sayings.

Talking about her, you will see a real spirit and enthusiasm inbuilt in her with a multi-talented personality may it be from drawing a picture or giving reality to writings from simple prompts with true facts and real-life stories with power and you would love to read it for sure.

INSTAGRAM:- _urvi_gajjar__

Hug..

I just wanted to give you a small gift
That is a tight hug
Hug is not just about meeting two bodies
Its about meeting two souls
Hug is not just a word its an emotion.

I want to give you a hug
Not just a hug but a tight one
Which can take your breath away
That makes you feel comfortable
Feels like someone is there for me
No matter what and makes you feel special.

A hug from the person you love the most
It can turn into a natural healing process
And that can reduce your stress level
Your anxiety, mood, irritation, sadness,and all
It can make you feel so relaxed
That you will always crave for that.

No matter whom you hug it can be anyone
Your parents, siblings, friends, soul mate
But the feelings you hold for that person
It does matters it's like you should feel that
You should always crave for that hug.

So never think its just a hug.
Always think a hug can change a lot
Its a painkiller for us
A feeling that you feel for someone close to you
And it can be only possible
When you are not diverted anywhere.

A hug can make you blush, smile, laugh,
Also can give a feeling of butterflies.

Nikhil Jain

Nikhil Jain is from Dhule, Maharashtra.
He loves to showcase his emotions through writing, and his hobby is a workaround.
He uses a simple language in his Shayari and poetry, which could be easily understood and which relates to every human.
He started writing due to lockdown.

INSTAGRAM:- Love.vibes143

चाहत है,

तुझे अपना बनाने की,
होठों पर तेरा नाम दोहराने की,
तेरी मुस्कुराहट में खो जाने की,
तेरे हर आंसू को पी जाने की,
हरपल तेरी यादों में खो जाने की,
मुश्किल में तेरी ढाल बन जाने की,
अंधेरे में रोशनी का दिया जलाने की,
तेरे नाम के साथ तेरा नाम जुड़ जाने की,
तेरे आगोश के दरमियान खो जाने की,
हर पल हर लम्हा तेरे संग बिताने की,
चाहत है तुझे जीवनसंगिनी बनाने की।।

Kristi Dutta

I'm Kristi Dutta . I'm a student . My first book as a co author was friendship. It's an amazing journey of writing. And writing is my secret talent .
INSTAGRAM:- krysty846

Love is a complicated thing in the world. Love can be with anyone like I love dogs, love cat and many more but main is "love can be with two persons" we people live for love. And yes we fall in love by chance and we stay in love by choice. When a boy and a girl love each other they don't love there body they love there heart . There heart beat for each other. Sometimes crush also converts into love. Jab mile do pyar ka laila aur majnu tab tab Zindagii banti ha suhani pyar mein do dil jab mile tab kuch to hua ,jab do dil ka takkar ho tab kuch to bomb blast hua ussi,ussi felling ko love kahte ha

Love is a complex. Love is full of emotions,trust, behaviour, respect, protectiveness , strong feelings. love is attractions... love means when two souls connect, two hearts connection..that's love. two persons feels that love. Because love is love and it's between two persons.

It was rainy day . I was on my way to home. Suddenly it rains so heavily , I walked faster .. my leg was slipped and I fell into my knees and he raised his hand. Not for an hour but for a second we both are looking each other's eyes..a sound was coming from our heart that this is your true love.

And when you get a a Sound from your heart then thinks this is your love you are finding whole the world..... Remember my words when you are going to choose your love for just a second wait and listen carefully what your heart says.

Vikrant Singh

Vikrant Singh is a 19 year old bsc student .
He is from Sonbhadra (u.p) .
He loves to write because writing is his passion .
He is the co - author of ' love without the knot ' and ' Unchained Thoughts ' .
INSTAGRAM:- __banna_sahab__

डर लगता है

सोचता हूं इज़हार कर दूं ,
सोचता हूं बंता दूं उसे की मैं उसे कितना
प्यार करता हूं ।
पर डर लगता है , डर लगता है ये सोचकर भी
की कहीं वो मुझसे दूर ना हो जाए ,
कहीं हमारी दोस्ती टूट ना जाए
डर लगता है ख्वाबों में भी तुझसे जुदा होने से
डर लगता है , क्योंकि एक ख्वाब ही तो है
जहा तु सीर्फ मेरी है
ख्वाब ही तो है जहा हमारी कहानी
हमेशा पूरी होती हैं
हकीकत ना सही तूं मेरे ख़्वाबों में तो है ।
डर लगता है ख्वाबों में भी तुझसे जुदा होने से ....

Tumhare Hone Ka Ehsas Laga Rehta Hai

Aaj bhi jab unknown no. se call aata hai
To dil me ek bechani si mach jati hai
Kyonki tumhare laut aane ka ehsas hamesa laga rehta hai ......

Ab mai station ke uss platform par nahi jata jispe tum pehli bar mili thi kyonki
waha tumhare hone ka ehsas laga rehta hai.......

Mai apni us shirt ko aaj bhi sambhal kar
rakhta hu jise pehan kar mai tumse pehli bar mila tha kyonki apni us shirt se tumhare khushboo ka ehsas laga rehta hai ....

Suchismita Ghoshal

Suchismita Ghoshal from Malda, West Bengal is an internationally acclaimed poet, professional writer, scribbler, published author, professional book critic, storyteller, columnist, former copy-editor at NotionPress Publishing, content writer, creative writing professional, nature lover and a change agent & former Worldwide Ambassadors' Coordinator for Global Youth Leaders Network. She is now a registered member of Global Youth Network. She cherishes her partnership with various publication houses of India & abroad. She enjoys working as a manager at Pen Brew Publishers. Suchismita also aims to heal people with the majesty of her words. She is an environmental activist too who brought reality to her dream as her debut book named "Fields of Sonnet ". Her recent releases are " Poetries in Quarantine" and "Emotions & Tantrums".
INSTAGRAM:- storytellersuchismita

Love 'Eleutheromania'

Some places have their own faces. Whenever we keep our steps there, it reminds us for someone special who has never gone blank from our mind. It's their smile which keeps us cozy in between a bunch of unknown faces. It's their memories that never leave us lonely & it's the moments we spent together which innocently warm our hearts. The most beautiful feelings are hidden in between the true promises & the honest determination of keeping them alive. I too have them!

The last time when it gave butterflies in my stomach was his hands strongly pressed against mine while we were in a cab, felt like in a cage full of freedom. We crossed miles after miles looking at each other for a round of intense gaze. We saw so many things dipped in our hearts. Revealed strange mysteries together. Travelling is always the best recreation for me but this was something unique. Travelling through each other's hearts & touching the eternal beauty weren't possible if it wouldn't be a "Love 'Eleutheromania' ". This word was discovered when I was writing a travelogue couple of months ago. Today I can intensely feel the 'Eleutheromania' in every inch of my life. I feel it for him, & want him to feel it back.

He said , "I love you."

A pair of shimmery eyes & a ring of warm breathe!

A short smile & a long pause!

That's it. I was more than fascinated.

Some words unheard & unsaid yet prominent through a long silence.

Leaving me speechless is always his tactics. I call him magician now-a-days for my brain rewinds all his words, promises, gazes, coziness & of course his sightlessness !

One month crossed when the last time he left a soft good-bye

kiss on my lips . I found it profound, just like old wine, gets better with age. It was something I can live for, something that can drench my soul in no time & something I was always in search of.

I didn't utter a word when he was in a gap then, a wall of window's thick glass, standing outside the cab, & bidding me goodbye. I too shook my hands & watched him slowly lagging behind & got vanished in a few seconds. My journey seemed to have a strange vacuum now. I couldn't long for him anymore as he had to go.

Strangely I'm in his city today, but not getting him by my side. He was one of the best 'Trouvailles" I've discovered through the journey of my life. I feel both blessed & lucky.

All I know he has successfully been able to put his face with my memory of this city. When we travel to a place & forget to have the best thing or eat the best food which is considered to be the significant thing about the place, it always leaves an empty feeling inside us & honestly, he has unknowingly secured that position for me.

I surmise the whole situation as a homesickness for someone I badly want to be with. It's an irresistible urge to make a journey to someone's heart & create a permanent abode.

I am in a voyage called love; let it be a part of puzzled forest, an endless sea, a mountain full of risky pinnacles, or whatever inevitable, my kind of adventure won't be fulfilled if I don't succeed in hitting the destiny named "him".

'Love' is an unending journey, encircled by the longest journey 'Life', & 'Eleutheromaniac' like me finds celestial happiness travelling in love like a nomad.

Our areas are small, not the world;

Just like our limited thoughts aren't enough in front of unending possibilities.

मनोज शर्मा

इनका नाम मनोज सदानंद शर्मा है और इनकी उम्र २० है । इन्होंने "मुंबई यूनिवर्सिटी" से अपनी "बी-कॉम" की पढ़ाई पूरी की है । ये अपने आप को लेखक तो नहीं कहते पर लिखते जरूर है । फ़िलहाल कविता, शायरी लिखते हैं और साथ ही साथ ग़ज़ल सिख रहे है।

INSTAGRAM:- mr._manoj_sharma

मुक्तक

मुझें अपनी मुहब्बत का अभी इज़हार करना है,
तेरी आँखों से ही मुझको तो आँखें चार करना है,
हुआ तेरा दिवाना मैं मुझे तू आजमा लेना,
तुझे तो वार करना है मुझे तो प्यार करना है ।

मुझें तेरी निगाहों ने कही है बात इक ऐसी,
अभी तक याद है मुझको गुजारी रात इक ऐसी,
बयां मैं भी नहीं करता बयां तू भी नहीं करना,
सही है इश्क़ अपना पर ग़लत है जात इक ऐसी ।

दो लाइन शायरी

मेरी मुहब्बत की बस इतनी सच्चाई होगी,
जहां तुम रहोगी वहीं मेरी परछाई होगी ।

तुम मुस्कुराओ और मैं भी मुस्कुराता रहूं,
इश्क़ जताओ तुम और मैं तुम्हें सताता रहूं ।

आप ग़र चाहती हो तो मार दो मुझें,
वरना मेरे हिस्से का प्यार दो मुझें ।

अब मान भी लो मेरा कहना मेरी जान,
साया बनके मेरे साथ रहना मेरी जान ।

Krishna Motwani

Krishna Motwani is a Student currently.
She use to pen down her feelings.
She is a moody girl.
She started writing in the month of june,2020.
She writes in her free time.
She writes some motivational quotes or poetries too and practices artworks also.
She lives her life like a bird
As bird flies freely and enjoys life like that she also lives her life freely and enjoy fullest.
INSTAGRAM:- unique__blog_

Unconditional Love!

I just don't know what should i talk to you,
I just don't know why I care for you,
But i know,
The one who makes my day joyful is only you!

सहा है।

सहा है मैने भी वो दर्द जो आज तुम सह रहे हो,
सहा हैं मैने भी वो चसके दूर चले जाने का दुख जो अब तुम सह रहे हो,
मेरी भी कोशिश थी उसे भूल जाने की,
रोया है मेरा भी दिल जैसे आज तुम रो रहे हो।

Jayashree Sahoo

Jayashree Sahoo is habitant of ODISHA .
Her writings started on yourquote,notojo and mirakee like writing platforms. You can search her on yourquote by name of Jaya Jayashree . Nowadays She is member of many writing communities and earned a alots of certificates through her writings .
She is Co.author of 140+ anthologies .Also She is Compiler of many anthologies in Hindi ,English and Odia languages . Currently She is working as project head and board member of a reputed publication .
According to her,if you dont express your inner feelings towards someone,then just write those on a paper and making yourself happy for without reason .
Also she has interested in singing ,travelling,photography also. Among of these extra activities She studying Nursing on govt medical and she has an aim for be a RN nurse and good writer .

INSTAGRAM:- mixing_of_emotions

I Love You More

I ll wait for u forever,
Just say me in loyalty ,
Do u love me in reality, ?
Somewhere I found many fake ,
So I don't want to do any mistake ,
If your love is true and pure ,
Don't proof it by doing better,
Just love me from your hearty inner,
It ll give me more and more pleasure,
You know I kept some surprises,
But I don't give you in easy case,
You have to be loyal and my half-better,
Then I ll trust you more than me in future,
I know attraction is so easy for falling in love,
But I think , somewhere hard trust with dedication is best more than love ,
So how much u attractive in outside ,that doesn't matter ,
Your sincerity and loyalty always matter forever ,
I wish I do love you daily in perfect pure ,
So at last just wanna tell you "I love you more "

Panalcherin Wekesa

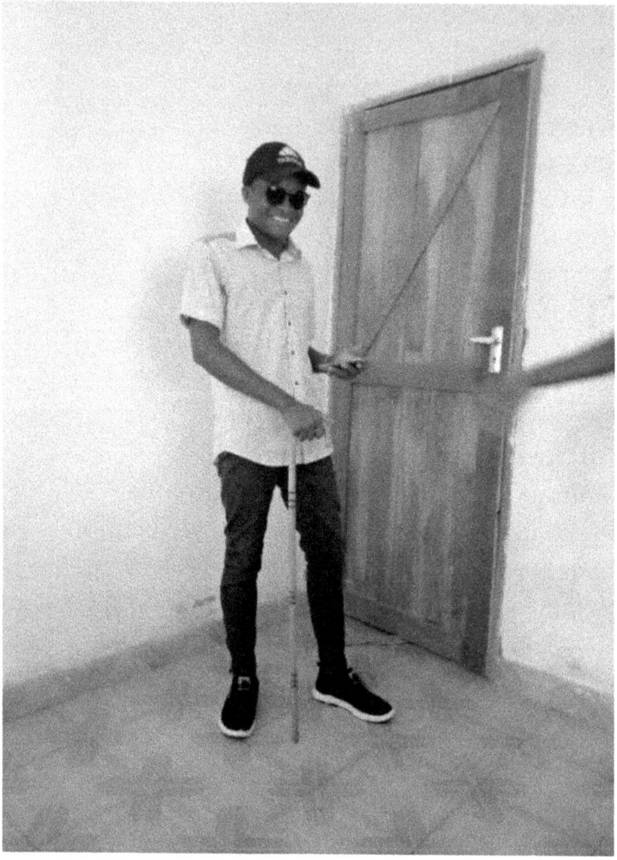

Palcherin is a Kenyan student who likes reading and writing

I Want You Back

My sword, armor and chariots are ready
Into the battlefield here I go
To kill, and with no mercy destroy
I want to go into the battlefield and fight
Because I want you back

I want to enter that deadly jungle
Be bruised, be injured and even be killed
I want to enter the deadly jungle and fight
Because I want you back

Into the deepest of forest I will go
Despite scorpions, beers and lions
I want to go into the forest and fight
Lose even my hands and legs
Because I want you back

I want to enter the ring and fight
Against giants and gigantic blows
I will stand like a man and fight
Lose everything with enthusiasm
Because I want you back

I want to go anywhere and fight
Because I hear your strained voice
I hear your heart calling on me
I'm here, I will fight everything that comes
Because I want you back

Ryan Sean

Prakhar Singh (AKA Ryan Sean) is a 21 year old Commerce Teacher from Sultanpur, UP. He is an Independent writer on Yourquote.Com. He had been writing short-stories and poem since age of 14. Some of his famous write-ups and poems are given below.
'Friendship or Love', 'Tales of Unsung Village' and 'Yes, I feel jealous' are some of his creations.
INSTAGRAM:- ryan_sean.88

Yes, I Feel Jealous.

When you're with your friends,
I feel jealous 'coz I'm not there.
When you're with your family,
I feel jealous 'coz I'm not there.
When you're with your relatives,
I feel jealous 'coz I'm not there.
When you talk someone else,
I feel jealous 'coz I want to be there.

Rain droplets fell on thy face,
I cry un-noticing and walk,
I wait and look at my phone before I sleep,
So that at least I can tell you my problems and talk,

After listening your voice I forget my worries,
You're the anaesthesia for my pain,
I want "you" to be drug overdose,
So that You can run in my veins,
These words are less to elaborate,
How I feel for you,
Just kind for your knowledge remember,
I am scar and my heels are you!

Tabassum Hasnat

Tabassum Hasnat, a freelance writer of shortform fictitious genres. She is currently completing her Pearson Edexcel Advanced Levels along with law and legal studies. She has co authored multiple international book compilations and anthologies, where her writeups have been published on platforms like Amazon, Kindle, Google books, Barnes & Noble and Notion press.

INSTAGRAM:- _tashaa8055_

One Such Tonic

Oh there you were,
one such tonic

bewitchingly brewing -
one of a kind tranquility

within my insides - but
it was time to withhold,
from swallowing you -

down my throat for often
you seemed to have -

poisoned the pits -
of my soul with an ardour,

that shouldn't once -
be enthralling me.

Love - A Rose, Love - A Thorn

It was that one coruscating
core such as that of yours

that had conspired somehow
to weave its way into the pits
of my soul stealthily

and as velvety as the petals
of some rose

until one day your warmth
smothered my insides as it

surreptitiously seeped out
of me leaving behind such
tormenting thorns of a love
that failed to thrive to adorn

every inch of me once and for all.

Rashmika

Rashmika is a voracious consumer of the written word, who always has a book (or a Kindle, keeping with times) by her side that she devours. She is, a student aiming to reach the peak and have a glimpse once. Rashmika moonlights as a blogger where her nostalgic side seeps through her words. She is inclined towards micro tales and poems but secretly harbours a dream of writing a novel.
INSTAGRAM:- rashmikaialfazz

Spring Days

I hope you find someone
who smiles at you every time you
walk in the door. Who finds beauty
in your scars. I hope you find someone
who never leaves you guessing. Someone
who lets you know for certain how they
always feel about you. I hope you find
someone who never hesitates to love you.
Who doesn't just give you pieces of their
time but it's eternity. I hope you find
someone who knows just how special you
really are. How your soul needs to be
loved. I hope you find someone who is
your biggest supporter. Who doesn't just
seek attention but gives it in return. But
mostly, I hope you find all of these things
in yourself first so that you can be
ready for this type of love…

Ashish Verma

Ashish verma is a software engineer. And he like to write shayari and poems .But he love to write sad shayari and poems.

INSTAGRAM:- ashish_verma4035

एक तुम्हारा होता था,एक मेरा होता था

कभी एक फ्रेम में दो मुस्कुराते चेहरे होते थे
एक तुम्हारा होता था,एक मेरा होता था

तुमको भी याद होगा
सन्डे-सन्डे एक साथ घूमने जाना
उस खामोश फिजां में जो आवाजें होती थी
एक तुम्हारी होती थी,एक मेरी होती थी।

तुम्हारे बालों में दो रंग के क्लिफ होते थे
एक तुम्हारे पसंद के,एक मेरे पसंद के होते थे

मैं तुम्हारी पसंद में खुश था
फिर भी तुम मुझसे मेरी पसंद पुछती
तो मुझे अच्छा लगता
यह भी सच था कि मैं तुझे कभी इनकार नहीं करता
लेकिन तुम भी तो मेरी हर बात मान लेती थी
दो अलग-अलग पसंद एक हो गए थे
तुम्हारी पसंद मेरी हो गई थी,मेरी पसंद तुम्हारे हो गए थे

तबियत मेरी बिगड़ती थी और खाना खाना तुम छोड़ देती थी
कहती थी तुम्हारा दर्द मुझे महसूस होता है
फिर तुम दूर क्यों गई
वापस आ जाओ ना
फिर एक डेस्क पे दो कप होंगे
एक तुम्हारा होगा,एक मेरा होगा
फिर एक कागज पे दो नाम होंगे
एक तुम्हारा होगा,एक मेरा होगा
फिर एक फ्रेम में दो चेहरे होंगे
एक तुम्हारा होगा,एक मेरा होगा

Hershey's

Even as a Young Child Hershey's would conjure up with stories with her imagination, sharing them with anyone who would listen. She have developed her storytelling and writing quite a bit since then, but the thrill of language and creation she first discovered as a child has never gone away. Get in touch if you've got any comments, questions, suggestions, or just want to say Hello. Hershey's would be more than happy to hear from you.

INSTAGRAM:- hiddenpartofmylove

Best Gift From God

Tanishq and Aarna were teenagers. And they were madly in love with each other. Tanishq was muscular, thin and tall. Whereas Aarna was a chubby short girl. But their physical appearance never mattered as they both were in love with Beauty of their Souls. And everyone believed it was a soulmate connection and admired the couple.

One fine day, Tanishq's friend said," Why don't you look for a beautiful and curvy girl? Aarna is fat and her face is full of Acne, she doesn't suit you."

After hearing this Tanishq calmly replied," Yes, my girl is fat and her face is full of Acne. But if she makes up her mind to become slim, she will definitely lose her weight and become curvy. As she is a teenager it's normal to have acne, and she can overcome it by getting treatment from a Dermatologist. Moreover as she gets older acne gets reduced. Aarna is beautiful, but not like those curvy girls whom you think and speak about. She is beautiful, for the way she thought, for that sparkle in her eyes when she talked about something she loved, for her ability to make other people smile even if she is sad. She is beautiful, deep down to her soul. And remember to see beauty of souls instead of bodies, your meaning and idea of beauty will be different."

After hearing this Tanishq's friend realised how pure and true their love was and told Aarna, " You have the Best Gift from God and that's Tanishq." To which Aarna replied," Yes, Best Gift I could ever get."

Parul Mishra

Parul Mishra was born at jabalpur, madhya pradesh on 18 th august 1997 . She was an amature writer. She tries to generate the love from pen and paper ...she Has worked for many anthologies one was with the great young writer Durjoy Dutta. At present she is working for " One step Ahead " her first anthology book . She is a writer ,poet and also a teacher of mathematics.

INSTAGRAM:- mishraparul_18 .

सालभर का प्यार

जनवरी में एक खाली किताब की तरह तेरा आना।
फ़रवरी की ठंड में भी तेरा गर्मी दे जाना।
मार्च में परीक्षा की तैयारी के लिये साथ में जगना।
अप्रैल में रिजल्ट की टेंशन में मूवी देख डालना।
मई की छुट्टी में हिल-स्टेशन पर जाना।
जून में उन यादों को फेसबुक-इन्स्टा में सजाना।
जुलाई में उस बारिश की हर बूंद में समा जाना।
अगस्त में दोनो परिवारों को मिलाना।
सितम्बर में शादी की तैयारी में उलझना।
अक्टूबर में तेरे उस अनकहे प्यार का पता चलना।
नवंबर में अपने इस रिश्ते को नज़र लगना।
और दिसंबर में इस किताब को अधूरी ही बंद कर देना।।

Hey You

Hey you,
You write from heart
You talk from heart
You decide from heart
But still says,
I never use my heart

Hey you,
You know I'm idiot
You know I'm mad
But still, You cares
But still, You love
That's why you are sweet

Hey you
Always be there for me
And make this bond so special

Hey you
You know I love you
So be there always for me

Pratham Mittal

He is very Positive, kind, helpful, friendly and happy soul. His passion is painting and writing. He has won many competitions, He has Been Co-Authored of 75+ Anthology and He has Been Compiler of 15+ Anthologies, and in the Process for more. He is an OMG Books Of Record Holder + Bravo International Book of World Record Holder for his Anthology Speaking My Truth. Participated in International Writing Competitions and Featured in Many Magazines & Newspaper also.

God's Gift

Love is sort of a river,
A never ending stream.
Love is shared by one another
To answer someone's dream.

It's a never ending story;
Love isn't a lie.
You can share altogether its glory,
For love will never die.

Love is all around you,
The moon and stars above.
Love may be a gift from God,
And God may be a gift of affection .

Diksha Motwani

Diksha is a passionate girl from Mumbai, Maharashtra. She loves to pen her feelings. She is introvert but her pen makes her extrovert. She is a writer, singer, artist and a poet!
INSTAGRAM:- radha_1229

आज भी याद है मुझे!

आज भी याद है मुझे तेरा वो बेवजह रूठना,
आज भी याद है मुझे किस तरह में पागलों कि तरह तुझे मनाया करती थी,
जब तू रूठता था तो जैसे मेरा रब ही रूठ जाता था,
आज भी याद है कि में तुझे किस तरह सीने से लिपटा लिया करती थी,
आज वहीं दिन मुझे सता रहे है,
तेरी यादों के सहारे जी रही हूं,
तू आएगा एक दिन वही दुआ किए जा रही है,
तेरा वह रूठना , मेरा वह मानना,
शायद ये ही है जो मुझे आज तेरे बिन सता रहा है।

Debarati Das

She strongly believes that one should never settle for something less than what one deserves and with this belief, she have come forward to be a part of this anthology.
She hopes that she will be getting all of our heartiest love and support throughout her journey.
Her writeups have been published in more than 100 national and international anthologies. She is really honored to be a part of this anthology and would like to extend her thanks of gratitude to all the members of this anthology and the readers as well.
INSTAGRAM:- debarati69

One Less Lonely Night

The stars over us kept shining so bright,
Looking at someone special gave me great delight,
The unspoken words in those eyes kept me standing upright,
We both proved to be in love at first sight.
The sudden gasp of wind touched me as a whole with immense pleasure,
Your presence felt to me more than an inexhaustible treasure.
One step by one step we came closer,
Our inner feelings got a stupendous exposure.
When you started invoking me to be highly versatile,
Somehow I started getting hypnotized by your affectionate smile.
We broke all the boundaries in love according to stereotypes,
Our utmost concern for each other was enough for our sorrow to get completely wiped.
It has been two years since we parted happily with each other,
Since then my heart has always convinced me to accept you as my elder brother.

Sakshi Sharma

Ms. Sakshi Sharma hails from Aligarh, U.P. She like to decorate her words and emotions on paper and has participated in various anthologies as co-author. She is biotechnologist and researcher by profession with more than 2 years of experience. Additionally, she is national kathak dancer. She wants to be unique! to stand out amongst the people and like to learn new things. She believes in delivering smiles on the faces.
INSTAGRAM:- ss.3684saki

हमें अंदाज़ा नहीं था

हमें अंदाज़ा नहीं था
की इस हाल में आ जाएंगे
तुम्हें समझते समझते, खुद को ही भूल जाएंगे,
हमने तो समझा तुम्हें, इस बेख़बरी में,
की न समझने का इल्जाम भी हम ही उठाएँगे,
हमें अंदाज़ा ही नहीं था, की इस हाल में आजाएँगे,
इक ख़ुशी की दरख़्वास्त की थी बस प्यार में,
क्या पता था गम की रियासतें ही नाम कर जाओगे,
क्यूं खता की हमारे पास आने की,
और अगर कर भी दी खता तो,
क्यूं मज़रत की इसे सुधारने की,
हम तो बस प्यार कर बैठे खुद से ही मुख़्तलिफ़ होकर,
क्या पता था हर प्यार की सज़ा सिर्फ हम ही उठाएंगे,
हमें अंदाज़ा नहीं था, की इस हाल में आ जाएंगे,
तुम्हें समझते समझते ख़ुद को ही भूल जाएंगे।

Srishty Singh

This is Srishty Singh. She resides from Jharkhand and currently doing her btech. She is a passionate writer who oozes out her emotion and thoughts through writtings. She has contributed to many anthologies as a co-author and took part in various contests and has volunteered many. She writes on inspirational and social topics and is a versatile writer.
INSTAGRAM:- srishty_28_singh

Heart

Dear heart,
you are my secret corner.
For all my pleasures and pain,
for all the losses and gain.
My bad time buddy and
good time companion.
Hold me when no one's there,
cheer me up and cherish me.
You are my secret mirror,
I see my inner beauty in you.
Whether my darkest, deepest side,
Or the part of me, pure and true.
Show me my true reflection,
Which defines you and the real me.
You are my happy place,
I rely on you for my being.
You are my secret corner.

Ananya Mohanty

Ananya Mohanty hailing from the city of Rairangpur. An author in 75+ anthologies and a compiler also. She is also a record holder in KALAM WORLD RECORD and SPECTRUM INSPIRING INDIAN WOMEN. Writing is like a way to say your feelings out. So I write to express myself . So some of the writing are in real my own stories. My life My story. I love writing for myself. This is also something I wrote from some of my life phase. My much of the writings are on romance, mystery, fantasy, motivation and horror.
INSTAGRAM:- Sweet_devil_lover

My Lovely Arranged Marriage

Today was a new start with my love,
The soul mates will become life partners.
It all started with a shy staring,
Ended with a wide smile.
Walking beside each other distantly,
Ended up holding hands.

Started with a simple shy nod in place of words,
Ended with vowing to each other.
Started taking steps on the new path,
Ended up at the end of aisle together.
It started with a simple fancy dress,
But ended up in a beautiful wedding dress.

It was my and your before,
But now it was our.
It was two bodies and two soul before,
Now it was two bodies but one soul.
It was just a normal day being myself before,
But its a fabulous day being our self now.

The new life is good,
But with love its awesome.
Having different opinions and taste may trouble,
But understanding each other will untangle every trouble.
A phase may be rough and toxic,
But supporting and being the backbone will make it healthy.

It was started by being complete stranger,
But ended up being twin flames.
It may be a deal at first,
But it is a wish now.
It may be an arranged marriage before,
But it is a love marriage now.

Abdul Hasan

Abdul Hasan is 17 years old. He is computer science student. He is from up (Ballia).He started writing qoutes, thaughts when he lost her friend. His fisrt evergreen quote together is -
"Ye Ishq bhi thand jaisi h,
Lg jae to bimar kr deti hai.
Kux riste toot jaroor jate,
Lekin kabhi khtm nhi hote."
And some qoutes dedicated to his loving one Angel. He is the Co - author of other books also - Treasure of Love, Carpediem.
INSTAGRAM:- Xtylish_dude_hasan05

Bardast nhi tmhe
kisi aur ke sath dekhna
Baat shaq ki nhi
Haq ki h.

Bhut kux badal gya
Meri Zindagi me,
Ek Tere aane ke baad
Ek Tere jaand ke baad.

Kamyab risto ka ek ussol hai
Bhul jao use Jo baate fizul hai.

Shikayte to khud se hai
Tmse to aaj bhi ishq hi h.

Ye Ishq bhi thank jaisi h,
Lg jae to bimar kr deti hai.

Kux riste toot jaroori jate,
Lekin kabhi khtm nhi hote.

Mahi Adlakha

Mahi is 15 years old. She belongs to a small town in Rajasthan. She writes out her heart.
INSTAGRAM:- dazzledust_

Are We?

There is a time at all times,
When all of you rhymes,
When the shadow of the sun,
Still brings sunshine,
And the song you murmur perfectly rhymes,
With u, with me,
Or with us,
I hope you stay forever this time,
Dear love, please rhyme,
Or maybe you just take another curve,
Is it just me,
Or are we all in love?

Is It Too Hard?

I'm an ocean full of emotions,
Just touch once with love,
And a wave comes your way,
I sent you one and kept waiting all day,
I didn't receive one till nine quarters,
Is it too hard to give a little push to the water.

Supriya Mukherjee

Supriya Mukherjee is a 19 years old girl, born on October 25th, 2002 in Ramgarh, Ranchi, Jharkhand. Currently She is pursuing BSc. in Biotechnology from Marwari College, Ranchi. She completed her 10th and 12th from Ramgarh.
She aims to become a researcher in her life so that she could contribute to nation. During her school life, she won gold, silver and bronze medals in Judo. It is actually a great achievement and due to that she carries spirit of sportsmanship which leads her to face every situation in a positive way.
She is very passionate about writing as she loves to express her feelings, experiences. She chose writing to express because she feels that words are very powerful way to give message to people, to share feelings and emotions and also to inspire people. She mostly writes about social issues, love, friendship, relationship and life.
She is very much active in social media platforms.
INSTAGRAM:- lillys._.words.

गर वो हासिल न हो पाया
तो खुद को एक इनाम देंगे

गर वो हकीकत न बन पाया
तो जिंदगी सपनों में बांट देंगे

है देख रखे हमने न जाने
क्या-क्या सपने मगर

गर वो साथ न दे पाया
तो जिंदगी तन्हा गुज़ार देंगे।

सीखा नहीं कुछ काम , तुझे याद करने के अलावा।
शामे बिताई नहीं , तुझपे मरने के अलावा।
यूँ तो देखा है कितने महफ़िलों में जाकर ।
मगर मिला नहीं जाम, तेरे होठो के अलावा।

Preetam Khatua

PREETAM KUMAR KHATUA, a native of Sambalpur, Odisha. A budding author and an adroit orator. Currently pursuing Bachelor in Dental Surgery in Bangalore. Loves to express heart's beat in words. Probably a romantic man of letters. Feel his poems and get lost in the world of delightfulness. Loves to define the beauty of a girl through words. Believes in works rather than sayings.

INSTAGRAM:- p.p_r_e_e_t_a_m

Apne kuch to khas h...
Ankahi kuch ehsas hai...
Mukhtasar apki hansi se mulakat h...
Noor-e-nafi apne alag hi baat hai...
Apne kuch to khas hai..
Khuli ho ya baand ho ankhen..
Bas apki mohtaaz hai..
Khusnuma har ek Ada apki...
Kuch alag Noor hai...
O-tarashe hue heere...apki betahasa chamak hai...
Kehta huun bas itna...
Ki aap me ek ehsas hai...
Kuch raaz hai...bas alag hi dastan hai..

Ruswa, Teri hansi ke dewane hazaron hain...
Banware, Teri mushkurahat ke parwane hazaron hain..
Pheeki wo phiza ..pheeka sab kuch..
Teri ek hansi ke age..
Mushkurahat aisi Teri ki mazboor hua chand bhi...
Guftugu-e-tariff karne ko..
Teri hansi ek shayari ...jise koi dohra nahi skta..mere Dil se isse koi mita nhi skta

Jane kyun Dil shayarana ho pada hai....
Rukshat Jo app huin, ye deewana ho pada hai...
Shayari to bas ek bahana hai...
Naam-e-wafa Tak..iss baat ko pahunchana hai...
Ki deewana huun mai apka..bas apka..

Apki aankhon m duub jaun...Meri mohabbat h..
Meri wafa ka shukrana...apki izzazat h...
Apki hoton ki mithas...ye Dil ki ibadat h...
Ye jahan ye mehfil sab sifr..Meri zununiyat h..

Mani Prasad Kar

Mani Prasad Kar lives in Jajpur. He is a person who loves to live his dreams . He is an emerging writer, a poet, a memer , and a free living guy . In his writings one can feel his emotions and visualize the words. He wishes to publish his own novel some day. He wants people to sense the aura of humanity and love through his writings. He looks forward for love from his readers .

INSTAGRAM:- Zephyr_of_woe

Stay A Little Longer With Me !!

Shall I compare thee to a summer's day?
Thou art more lovely and more temperate:
Rough winds do shake the darling buds of May,.
: William Shakespeare

"What is love ? " one of the most fascinating question yet an unsolved mystery. Poets compare it to the beauty of nature , painters paint it with all the colours , a writer pens it down with emotion and a heart broken illustrates it as a hell. It is that feeling which is worshiped by God themselves . Love is that balmy music which on hearkening gives us the sense of piousness.

And ask me ,Mani what is love ? I will say nothing but "she " . This pronoun, what I learnt in grade one defines my life now. " she" the most beautiful word in dictionary and the most winsome part of me.

I meet her after a month of Me getting into Delhi Institute of Medical science. It was a complete new place but thanks to my mixing conduct and my love for basketball which helped me to make a lot of friends both of my batch and seniors . I was a new lad joining the first year so even friends could not help me from being ragged. Now when I look back I fall in love with that ragging too. Strange right ! Ha-ha.. let me explain you. It was an usual evening . I was playing basketball with my seniors and the ball pounced up the fence of our court. Being the junior I had to fetch the ball from outside. I ran out drenched with sweat . And I saw a group of girls standing near the cafeteria , one of them was yelling with the ball in her hand and most probably it had hit her. I couldn't see her face but could sense her anger . I went there calm and quiet with an apologizing face . I said in a low voice , " It's our ball " . The moment I said she turned towards me . And her turning turned my life upside down.

There was “she” . Her eyes were so pulchritudinous that I was transfixed to it. It seemed as if time had paused for me . I could here my heartbeat clear and getting faster . It was like I could here her screaming but that scream seemed words of love from her beautiful peach red lips. I was literally thrown aback to a beautiful hallucination from which I would never want to come back. But suddenly I was back to my senses with her question , “ Hey !.. am talking to you .. you belong to which year ?”. I fumbled a bit and answered I am from first year . She rebuked saying , “ Don’t you know how to respect your senior .. I guess u need to call me ma’am..” . I said sorry Ma’am . I explained her how the ball came out . They started laughing ,may be due to the unusual way I explained with . One of them said now take the ball and go, be careful next time but she resisted it by saying no first hold your ears and do 10 sit-ups and then take your ball . That was a huge embarrassment when everyone was looking at you especially girls. But that day I was so lost in her eyes that I started doing it . I was looking straight into her dainty eyes ,most of the time our eyes matched and she would lower them down . My task was over, they returned my ball and went away . But why I felt like she would turn and look at me and guess what she did turn and there was a ting of smile on her lips. I still remember that smile of her , it was just love. I was so much attracted to her that I would imitate her every where she goes ,may be its library or cafeteria and even corridors . And let me tell you she looked the most alluring and cute at the temple where she used to do prayers. It went on for some days I had never got that much courage to talk to her. It is not that she didn’t notice me but never asserted. One day she was sitting in the cafeteria. I was there looking at her from the table in front. She stood up and came to the table I was sitting . I was dumbstruck . She ordered two coffee and asked me , “ what is going on ?” I said in a shivering voice , “ nothing ma’am ..” . She answers it with clinched eyes, “Do

you think am unknown to the fact that you are following me since that day and you look straight at my eyes" Her eyes lowered as she says it with a mischievous cute smile. I knew I was caught red handed and replied negatively. In the mean time the waiter showed up with the coffee. She with lowered eyes pushed a cup towards me along with a question " Mani.. don't lie , ok ! say you don't love me ? ". And believe me it felt like my heart stopped for a second, my mind came up with many questions like how she knows my name?, is she also stalking me ? , What does this cute smile mean ?. Within all these dilemma an involuntary answer came out of my mouth in oblivion , " I love you.. I love you from the very day I saw you.. I am in love with your beautiful eyes comely smile and infact everything .." . She was looking straight in my eyes .. her eyes lowered again with a lovely shy filled smile and a soft voice said , " never leave my hand " .. Days rolled by we both were falling deeply in love with each other, in fact we both are dwelling inside each other. Everything was going good. I was selected for a speech on the occasion of World Health Day for which I had to travel to AFMC to be a part of two days camp. I was practicing my speech in front of her, a few hours before I was about to leave , that she fainted with a bleeding nose . I panicked and rushed her to the emergency ward. After a few minutes she came into senses. The doctor prescribed MRI scan of brain and some other tests. I had by that time forgotten my speech but she held my hand with a low voice and said , " oye ! Stupid go to your competition nothing has happened its just a common thing " I firmly said no but she gave me her promise for which I had to unknowingly go . I hugged her tightly, she too held me tight.. tears rolled down my eyes. She told in my ears ," Now go , I will be waiting with flowers to celebrate your win " I was not willing to leave her . She wiped out my tears and with a smile said ,go. I went unwilling and to make her happy I gave my best, got the gold medal and came

running to share my triumph. As I stepped in the college I saw a huge gathering of students . There was some one covered with white bed sheet and flowers . My heart was shrinking down . My eyes were searching for her when it came across her photo with a garland of flower . I was in deep trauma, I was crying like a little baby, I had lost my everything but She had kept her promise she was with flowers waiting for me . I placed the medal near her feet and was moving back that her mother hands me a hand written letter that quotes…
“ STAY A LITTLE LONGER WITH ME !!”

Archishman Satpathy

Archishman Satpathy, often called "The Enthusiast Writer" is a young dynamic guy from Deogarh, Odisha, is a young lad of 17.

He is the co-author of 300+ Anthologies and Author of the book "LAKEEREIN ZINDAGI KE".

He is the Brand Ambassador of an world record holder antho of NLHF, the Brand Ambassador and the Marketing Head of the Roses and Quills Community, the Coordinator of The Unicorn Tales, the Editor of The Sturdy Writers Community, Chief Operating Head of Gleaming Inscription Community, Chief of Hindi Department of InKadhai Publication, English Jury of Writers Ammulet.

He is the Co-founder of The Peaceful Writers Community and The Writing Gurus Community.

He is currently in 20+ Writing Communities at present.

He won the "Youngest Writer to 200 Anthologies" award by Indian Professional Awards.

INSTAGRAM:- jokerpoet_2882

Loving You Was Sunshine

Loving you was a lovely sunshine
Some gusty feelings far apart
Some perfect colab so condign

Remembering our voyage in that spline
When we were no souls promised
As of now we are ready for the sail
Lets be of each other so divine

I still remember those days when
I missed out looking for yours
Somewhere in the corners of zion
And anywhere in search of yours

Just then we have whine for each
And for sometime the door said pause
But I do remember how we care for each
For reline each others dream destiny

May be our love is so special
That am able to compare with sunshine
It will be scripted in books of history
People will celebrate our holy shrine ,

First Love In Zion

I met my first love in the Zion
There I felt what if in the globe
Thought whether souls can interpret
Just then thought the way we lived
Can the love be immortal or else
It will be just an eye-catching moment
With an unfurnished heart so stiff
Shall I promised for Valentine's luck
The greatness hidden within is still
A charming unknown to her soul mate
But I want to be divine in your soul
The flowers of heaven now showering
In the fountain of our soulful linking
The attachment is now strengthening
And trust me is being now unbreakable
The endearment of intimacy is lived
The proclamation of love hunt continued
May be I will fall, I will be challenged
But I assure I will never leave the field
I will love you with immortality of heaven

Surekha Wankhede

Surekha Wankhede belongs to Orange City, Nagpur, Maharashtra. She is persuing her graduation in B. Pharmacy course from RTMNU University. She writes in every type of genre, which considering where you are reading this, makes perfect sense. She's the best known for English poetry. She writes on every topic, she looks most innocent girl but her mind is filled with lots of creative and interesting stuffs. Passionate about her work, in love with her family and dedicated to spreading joy and light of her uniqueness. She is working as PH and Head Of The Magazine Dept. at The Opus Coliseum Publication. She wrote her magic just like the chemistry.

INSTAGRAM:- nuance_sayings
surekha_wankhede

One Sided Love

One day, he came beside me,
The inner me gives the perfect answer.
I started looking at him,
He was unaware about it.
When I saw him,
There's an affection towards him in my heart.
It's like one sided love.
But we won't act like that.
Because we both have started loving each other deeply.
But we are not ready to express our feelings for each other.
Sometimes we forget rest of the things and we stare at each other like we are gazing the beauty of moon.

Riddhi Gupta

Riddhi is a Delhi based poet who is currently a student. She is utterly enthusiastic as well as zealous about writing poems and considers writing as a medium to express her thoughts and emotions. She is immensely fond of writing poems on nature. Along with that she is also passionate about clicking pictures that depict the beauty of our environment!
INSTAGRAM:- Thestargazingsouls

Belong To You

Like a flower in your arms,
Delicate and gentle,
I demand nothing but us,
You and me wrapped up in a blanket,
A heart full of love, full of trust!
The Milky Way, the bewitching stars,
All reminding me of you,
Even if we're light years apart,
This girl, this heart, belongs to you!

Fireflies' Flame

Beneath the luminous stars,
Dancing amidst the fireflies in June,
Lost in each other, Laughing and smiling,
Hearts overflowing with love, so pure!
Fingers entangled, the dazzling eye contacts
Everything seems perfect, life's back on track,
Under the glow of the fireflies' flame,
You and me, our ultimate aim!

Ganesh Sadashiv Patil

This Is Ganesh Sadashiv Patil From Jalgaon,Maharashtra.He Is The Student Of UG In Field Of Pharmacy.He Is Writer And Poet Who Writes 100+ Poetry In Hindi And Marathi Languages.He Has Worked In 10 Anthologies As A Coauthour.He Is Also Been Part Of Pratibha E Magazine.He Is Also Been Part Of Various Poetry And Writing Competitions At National Level.He Loves To Write On Love,Humanity, Motivation And Social Themes. He loves to write down his feelings, his thoughts.He Is The CoAuthor Of 20+ Anthologies.

INSTAGRAM:- gsp9599

चॉकलेट सा प्यार

जिंदगी हम दोनो की ऐसी है की हो बंद किया हुआ चॉकलेट का खजाना
खुशबू और मिठास फैलती है उसकी जब खोलता है कोई उसेही अपना
आपके शब्दोमें है वो मिठास जो एक तुकडेके खानेसे हमे मिल जाती है
मन भी हमारा हो जाता है प्यारा आपसे मिलकर बात कुछ खास होती है
गुस्सा हो या फिर प्यार हो आपका बस लगता है हमे अब मिठा भरा प्यार
बोलकर आपसे करना चाहते है हम हमारे इस प्यार के रिशते का इझहार
देखकर इस चॉकलेटको करिबसे हमे भी आ जाती है बस आपकी हि याद
ना जाने कैसी ये डोर बंद गयी है ऐसी इस चॉकलेट के मिठास की है साद
दिल ये हमारा भी एक चॉकलेट हो गया है मिलना आपको चाहता है आज
आप हमारे इस प्यारभरे एहसास को जान लो यही है बस हमारी एक आस

Kinjal Patel

किंजल पटेल

किंजल पटेल, आनंद गुजरात से है। एस. पी. युनिवर्सीटी, विध्यानगर से बी.कॉम और सोमनाथ युनिवर्सीटी से पीजीडीसीए किया है। अभी दस साल से हाइ-टेक कंम्प्युटर, बोरसद मे एक़ रिसेप्शनिश्ट है और टैली एकाउंट पढ़ा रहीं है। इन्होने 25 से ज्यादा Anthologies मे contribute किया है। और compiler भी है। इनका मानना है हर हाल में खुश रेहना क्योंकि जिंदगी दोबारा नहीं मिलती, वो बीते पल भी दोबारा नहीं मिलते। आपको जिंदगी मे कुछ मिले या ना मिले पर फिर भी कोशिश जारी रखनी चाहिए। क्या पता कहीं किसी मोड़ पर अपनी मंजील मिल जाये। लिखना इनका शौख है।

"मुझें पढ़ पाना हर किसी के लिये मुमकिन नहीं मैं वो किताब हुं जिसमे शब्दों की जगह जजबात लिखे है।

INSTAGRAM:- Kinnu_patel226

Real_in_unreality

कैसे जाने दू तुझे

कैसे जाने दू तुझे
तुने तो मुझे जीना सिखाया है,
अपने हक़ के लिए लड़ना सिखाया है।
तुने मुझे दिल खोलकर हँसना सिखाया है,
तुने हर हाल मे खुश रहना सिखाया है।

कैसे जाने दू तुझे,
तुने सच्चे प्यार का अर्थ समझाया है,
तुने बेवजह मुस्कुराना सिखाया है।
तुने तो सपने देखना सिखाया है,
तुने इन्सान पहचान ने का सलिका सिखाया है।

कैसे जाने दू तुझे,
तुने क्षमा देना सिखाया है,
तुने स्वाभिमान से जीना सिखाया है ।
तुने हर दर्द मे मेरा साथ दिया है,
मेरी हर परेशानी को सुलझाया है।

कैसे जाने दू तुझे,
मेरी हर नाराज़गी को मनाया है,
मेरी हर ज़िद को पूरी की है।
तु ही तो मेरी ताकत और,
तु ही तो मेरी कमज़ोरी है।

कैसे जाने दू तुझे,
तुम मेरे जीने की वजह हो,
तु मेरा सच्चा प्यार हो।
तुम मेरे दिल का करार हो,
तुम मेरी जान हो।

तेरे बिन

आज मेरा जिस्म से कोइ टुकडा अलग हो रहा है...।
आज इस भीड मे दिल अकेला महेसूस हो रहा है...।।

क्यों जा रहे हो मुझसे इतना दूर....।
नहीं जियां जायेगा तुम्हारे बिना एक भी पल...।।

क्या यें मोंसम भी है साथ मेरे ...।
जो भी बरस गया इस फैसलै सै तेरे...।।

कहीं मन नहीं लगता तुझसे बात किय़े बिना...।
आंखे अब भी ढुंढ रहीं है तुझे आसपास कहीं...।।

मेरां चांद मुझे मेरे पास चाहिए...।
ना की उस आसमान में बादलो के बीच...।।

जिंदगी हो तुम मेरी, सांसे हो इस रूह की,
जरूरत हो तुम मेरी, धड़कन हो तुम मेरे दिल की,

तुम बिन कैसे जिये, कैसै रहैं तुम बिन...।
सदियों सी लगती है रातें, सदियों जैसे दिन।।

कहीं से भी लौटकर वापस आ जाऔ...।
नहीं जियां जाता यैं एक पल भी तुम्हारे बिना...।।

Vedika Shukla

Vedika is an aspiring Delhi based poet who is currently a student. She loves to express herself and connect with others through her writing. She also has a keen interest in photography and especially loves clicking pictures of the sky!
INSTAGRAM:- thestargazingsouls

A Broken Heart

You left me, you broke my heart years ago,
But at night I still live it all again,
All my efforts of escaping the painful memories of you and me in vain,
I act like I'm sane,try to hide my insanity but in the end that just adds to my affliction,
Ever since you left,
This habit of inflicting agony on myself has become a sweet addiction.

I need this to end,the pain,the suffering,the demons,
I need it all to go away,
I don't think I belong here and without you by my side I wouldn't wanna stay anyway!

Fate

What do you see when you look at the night sky?
Millions n millions of stars can be seen,
All of them have a story to tell,
Infinite possibilities of infinite different realities,
Tell me do you believe in alternate universes?

Do you believe in fate?
Cause if you ask me I'd say yes,
Me n you sitting here today beneath the beautiful sky was written in the stars
And right now I'm in my most vulnerable state trusting you enough
As to not hide my scars,
And before the whole universe to see,
In this moment I'm telling you how much you mean to me!

Merlin Dorcus

Merlin Dorcus is an educator and a research scholar. She is raised in the Manchester of South India. She is the co-author of many anthologies. She is a writer who pens soulful words dipped in the ink of love. She inks to give soul to words and life to emotions. According to her, 'Poem, blooms from the spark of happiness or from the broken pieces of sadness'. She unleashes her greatest wishes through her musical words.
INSTAGRAM:- merlinish_inked_solace.

Being Alone

I am so alone that no one is here
To care or share my despair.
Thinking about the rolling years
Filled me with so many fears,
Night shades veiled my room by
Making my eyes so dry.
Memories of you makes me glad
Your absence makes me sad,
With you my world disappears
Consuming the darkness of the spheres;
My heart echoes my deep isolation
Leaving me in a pool of sad emotion.
What I need is your gentle arm
With love to feel your warm,
Like the fog that had flown
You left me all alone.

Nilanjana Sarkar

Author Nilanjana Sarkar hails from West Bengal, Alipurduar and currently she's studying in class 12 and worked as an head of the Publication in WYIMUN on based on the three committee WHO, UNHRC and UNDP. She has also worked as an Entrepreneur with team Elite which deals with E-commerce, direct selling and social media platforms, she has already completed her internship in marketing by UNLEASH YOUR PASSION, she has been awarded as Extraordinary talent award on 2020 by Star and Genius book of record,her article had also get published and features over Indiatalks.org and yourstartups.in as a celebrity Author, she's is very hardworking and passionate girl and loves to do creativity through her writing, she mostly writes on erotics stuffs as well as on many topics which helps her to explore her more and more. She is a public speaker as well as a motivational speaker. She is an impulsive writer who oozes out her emotions and feelings and thoughts via writing.

INSTAGRAM:- _nilanjanaaa

Love Of A Dew Drop

In this chilly winter night
I was a drop of dew in the dark
You were fresh leaf of the morning
A new chapter was about to start

I was a cold water droplet
You were a sack of warmth
Slowly night grew to gloomy
Stars were afar

After so long year's of waiting
I reached your soul
Adoring the beauty of yours
I smiled so true and fresh

Something different the weather was
I forgot to reflect the sky
Thoughts piled up with your presence
It was only you in my reflection

So madly in love, I was
So perfectly you played on
I hoped for a new day to come
You deceased me in the dark hemisphere

The fresh leaf of you
Became dank and stinky
I choose to stay upon you
But you poured me down hastily

Down the lane of love
You were a deceptive mask
And finally in your love
I lost my existence

Arun Pratap Singh

This is Arun Pratap Singh from Agra, and currently he is studying in third year bcom, he loves to write express his thoughts and emotions. He is very hardworking and loves to to express himself more and more through writings.
INSTAGRAM:- arun_pratap11

Love is real but more real with the right person that's why she is the only lady I want to drink more than oxygen. The lady who became my persona some years ago after she saw me scanning the whole crowd and it was her wall of beauty and smile that was blocking my thoughts. For once I could taste the real love in the air around her and nothing could prevent me from loving her neither rich men,friends ,alcohol nor drug's. Or maybe it was the bond which was untold?

With endless bullet's from her heart she kept shooting them at me and the only worry is that to date i keep bleeding love for her. My heart cemented to hers with no regrets of having exploited such opportunity. She keeps tying my loose ends and loving her was never a crime . My first source of inspiration to write words that rhyme. People do extraordinary things for hatred but she has kept doing greater things for our love. Forever be my sun to always threaten my skyline.

Irene Joseph

She is Irene Joseph from Kerala, currently doing her triple degree course in Rajagiri college. Her life has given her a lot of experiences that she wanted to express it out. But the society has curbed all her emotions, like the retreating waves. Now she is brave, for she has her power in words, through words she communication every possible thing;for art is immortal.

INSTAGRAM:- locked_heart_voices

Weeping Rose

Where would I go,
For I am nothing without you..
Is rose a flower, or a weapon,
For it pierces in, into the flesh
Bath in the blood, for retaining the colour..
My life was colourful,
Just as how rainbows are..
I need the colour once more,
Holding it in my hand, I feel the pain
Of happiness, not attained..
For I give you my blood coloured Rose
Come back to me, as I weep alone..
For the pain I feel
Is mine and the rose..
Waiting, wanting, watching
By the valley, for I know
You will come back to me..
I hope..

My Heart For Her

Through all the flaws,
The coldest ice ever.. Melts
As one of a kind, the heart
Frozen out, but beating hard
To provide the warmth that never felt..
Then saw a spot in the black canvas,
But not a spot in white..
The Moon light's the darkest passage
For Sun is brightest.. But
Moon precious, as of a diamond
It reflects the rays… fallen on her
His love… Her life

Shaik Moiden S

Shaik Moiden S is an profound writer from Chennai he wrote thousands of quotes ,short stories and poems . He is passionated on writing
And we personally wish all the very best for his efforts
INSTAGRAM:- Quote_writer_90skid

Ask me to describe my love for you and I will tell you this: Trying to describe my love for you is like asking someone to describe what water tastes like it's impossible to do and it's impossible to live without you.

Love isn't a choice made, its the way we were created to be. Love shared is untold, it is something for everyone to see. Love is found by faith in it and by those don't throw it away. You are a precious part of my heart and that is where you will always stay.

Kirti Goel

Kirti Goel is a 15 years old ambitious girl. She is a class 9th student and She is from Ambala Cantt, Haryana. She is a passionate Poet who believes that words can make up the feelings!! She is the co-author of 20+anthologies out of which 15 has been published. She is the compiler of 5 books and is working on her solo book as well . She is also been regarded as the National Record Holder . Her pen name is Kalamqueen. And her evergreen lines from her quotes are…

"रिश्ते उम्मीद और जिंद पर टिकाए जाते है जनाब , खून का रिश्ता तो बस एक बहाना है"!

INSTAGRAM:- Kirtigoel24

Larly's Lost Love

Another day,
An eye harks blue,
And as I stay,
beyond your view..

I remembered your care,
going through my hair,
your beautiful smile,
just hypnotize me for a while!!

So soon I die,
Must my soul fly,
But I'll keep love you,
So in the sky ..

V.Dhanashree

Hello reader, she is V.Dhanashree from India living in the state called Tamilnadu in Chennai city. She is pursuing my undergraduate degree in History in Women's Christian College, Chennai, Tamilnadu. She is a simple and passionate writer who loves to write essays, poems and quotes in an easy and understandable manner so that it directly reaches the hearts of every reader. Her goal is to create a dignified society that spreads peace and kindness by eradicating poverty and illiteracy everywhere around the world. She strongly believes that writing is an extraordinary weapon to change the world to a better place to live in for all lives without any variations and discriminations.

Think Before You Leave

Love is a beautiful emotion between true souls. Trust and loyalty are the symbols of pure love. One should be able to accept the other wholeheartedly with affection and kindness. The past and present of a person should never influence you to judge that person in a wrong way. A true companion is the one who does not care about your past but willingly takes care about your present and future. Truth is the basic building block of every form of love in the world. If you are honest to your partner, then your love will definitely be an everlasting love. Nowadays many relationships come to the edge of withdrawal because their is lack of communication and a lot of misunderstandings between the partners. Above all, situations and circumstances make a person lie to their partner which finally results in a great clash. When you unconditionally love a person, you need to have patience and give some space to your partner too. Meanwhile, when it comes to a relationship, you need to think more than a hundred times before you could make a decision. You have to remember that your decisions not only affect you but also your partner's life and career. Before you could conclude your love, give it another try to sit and talk politely with your partner. Spend some time to listen to your partner's invaluable words and it will really make a magical change in you!

" Love is never complicated, because it's easy."

Anshuk Dwivedi'ranghin’

अठ्ठावीस वर्षीय अंशुक द्विवेदी'रंगहीन' श्रीमती उषा-डॉ. रमेश द्विवेदी की पुत्री है।मूलतः ग्राम धतुरिया,क्षिप्रा तट इंदौर(म.प्र.) भारत से है।वर्तमान में कनाड़िया,इंदौर में निवास करती है।हिंदी संस्कृत साहित्य से एम.ए. द्वयं करने के पश्चात बी.एड कर अध्यापन कार्य में प्रवत्त हैं।परम्परागत पारिवारिक ज्योतिषीय कार्य में संलग्न रहकर ज्योतिष कार्यालय संचालित करती हैं।इनके पोएटार्डस का संकलन "ज़ियारत" भी writersgramm appपर उपलब्ध है।छ अन्य सांझा काव्य संकलन"love without the knot, Treasure of love,SHE,A men's hidden emotions,प्रस्तावनाUnchained thoughts,The Wrinkle in time प्रकाशित हो चुके हैं।अन्य SHE The Mahakali,अहसास तेरे मेरे,last message,The tears we remember,वंदेमातरम,Aasma,Thrones and Roses,My love is gone,Rashmi,Hum Hindustani,Fog of Heart,Neacked Flower,The Versatile World,Euphoric World,long road to go,Tales of heart,EffectofEternity,SecretAdmirers, Nice&Spice,The Marked paper,The Gun in dusk,Battle of emotion,महा शिवाय में सह लेखिका के रूप में कार्य कर रही है।वर्ष २००४ से काव्य साधना में रुचि रखती है।इनकी कविताओं से जुड़ने के लिए इनके यूट्यूब चैनल#Anshukranghin से जुड़ा जा सकता है।

INSTAGRAM:- anshuk_ranghin

तू मेरा

तेरे कांधे पर सर हो मेरा,
तू है सबका मगर हो मेरा।
मैं ना राधा न हूँ रुक्मणी,
फ़िर भी हो गिरधर मेरा।
तेरे साथ जहाँ हो खड़ी,
बस वहीं पर हो घर मेरा।
तेरी आँखों से हुआ जो शुरू,
तेरी बाँहों तक सफ़र मेरा।
जैसे आँख का हो आँसू कोई,
हो तो हो गिरधर मेरा।
मीरा भी मैं न बन सकूँ,
तब भी हो नागर मेरा।
मैं अवनी बनूँ सबकुछ सहूँ,
बस तू बन जा अम्बर मेरा।

सितारा

मैं वो सितारा नहीं जो टूटकर
ख़्वाहिश पूरी करूँ।
मैं आफ़ताब बनकर
तेरी दुनिया रोशन करूँ।
तू माहताब बन,
मुक़म्मल न सही।
कहकशाँ में सितारों
की कमी तो नहीं।
पहाड़ कटेगा ये हिज्र का,
मेरे अश्क़ों की नमी से।
क्या फ़र्क़ पड़ता है अब,
आदमी को आदमी से।
अब चांद मेरे रास्ते में है,
तो क्यूँ तमन्ना अधूरी करूँ।
हर ख़्वाब में तुझसे मिलकर,
रोज़ कम कुछ दूरी करूँ।

Chirag L Sagar

Chirag L Sagar is a 1st year MBBS student studying at Srinivas Institute of Medical Sciences and Research Centre,Mangalore. His hobbies are poetry, reading - books,novels, autobiographies,philately, listening to songs,sports like cricket and badminton,cooking. He is a medico by profession and a writer by passion. His dream is to become an Oncologist and a successful writer.

INSTAGRAM:- chirag_cls18

To Being Yours Forever

My heart resonates with yours when I take a breath,
And I realize that you're right next to me.
Even though we're miles away from each other,
Your thoughts sway in my mind every single moment,
And I feel that you're right next to me.
A day without you feels like an year,
And I turn dull and gloomy.
When I feel your presence,
My heart's floating in cloud nine.
Wish you were next to me.
I'd love to spend my whole life alongside you,
And finally take a last breath holding your hand.
My existence in this world,
Is not at all a coincidence.
I've always had a person in my life,
Whom I love beyond the moon and back.
If I lose you anytime, anywhere,
I'll go against all odds and fight with the world,
To win you back.
The dark rain clouds in the sky,
Are bound together by the threads of love.
The gentle shade that comes up after a round of torrential rain,
Is a creation of the Almighty to cheer you up.
I dream of nothing,
But staying besides you holding your hands,
Live my life with you,
Until my last breath.

Flairs and Glairs, a platform by a student for the students. We are esteemed youth struggling to carve out our path for our future and we follow a basic mindset Since everyone is not born with all-round skills. Joining hands with people who are born to execute it with perfection is the best way to evolve. Self-Evolution is the need of the hour but, evolving as a community is what we strive for. The initiative as kickstarted by, Founder- Mr. Shubham Shah with the motive to utilize the skillset and talent of writing has now a team of 10+ people who are actively participating into newer forms of learning and discovering talents among youngsters. We Provide platform and services like Publishing opportunities, Open mics, Workshops, Hands-on training. Operating with Brand Name of Flairs and Glairs (Publication House), we offer the chance of elevating a passionate writer to an esteemed author With Brand name Teekhe Zasbaaat. We bring to you an opportunity to get accustomed with the Public Speaking and Presenting of Thoughts along with regular challenges to brush up your inking spirit. The newest initiative to extend our services we introduced in a new writing Platform- The Glittering Fables and Ink Over Tears.

We Choose to Fly Like A Falcon than to be

a Leg Pulling Crab.

To Know More: Infoline – 7781900870
Mail Us At-
flairsandglairs@gmail.com / info@flairsandglairs.in
Or Visit is at
www.flairsandglairs.com / www.flairsandglairs.in
Social Handles- @flairsandglairs @teekhezasbaaat\

www.ingramcontent.com/pod-product-compliance
Ingram Content Group UK Ltd.
Pitfield, Milton Keynes, MK11 3LW, UK
UKHW022005190726
13853UKWH00004B/1745

9 789391 302207